The Uncorker of Ocean Bottles

WRITTEN BY Michelle Cuevas

ILLUSTRATED BY Erin E. Stead

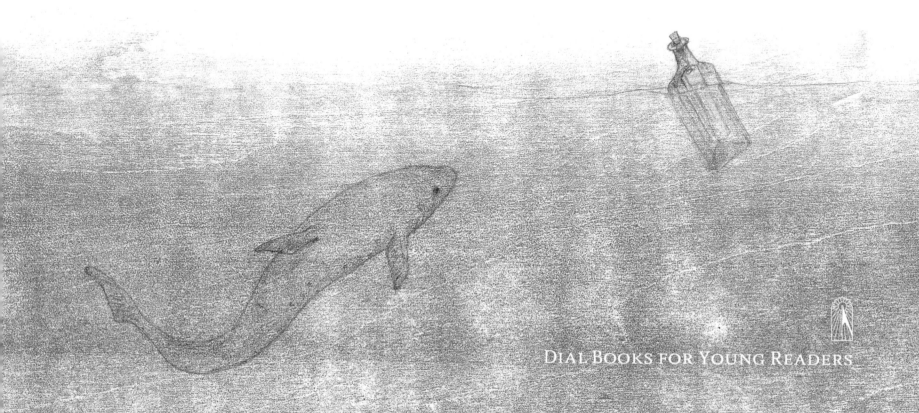

DIAL BOOKS FOR YOUNG READERS

For the Ocean Bottle Senders and Ocean Bottle Seekers:
Try. Want. Wish. Tell.
—M.C.

For my mom
—E.E.S.

Dial Books for Young Readers
Penguin Young Readers Group
An imprint of Penguin Random House LLC
375 Hudson Street
New York, NY 10014

Text copyright © 2016 by Michelle Cuevas
Illustrations copyright © 2016 by Erin E. Stead

Printed in China
ISBN: 978-0-8037-3868-3
10 9 8 7 6 5 4 3 2
Design by Lily Malcom
Text set in Fiesole

The art was made using woodblock prints, oil pastels, and pencil.

THE UNCORKER OF OCEAN BOTTLES lived alone on a high spot with only one tree for shade. He always kept his eyes on the waves, watchful for a glint of glass.

He had a job of the utmost importance. It was his task to open any bottles found at sea and make sure they were delivered.

Sometimes to deliver a bottle, he needed only to stroll to the nearest village.

Other times, he would journey until his compass became rusty and
he felt loneliness as sharp as fish scales.

Sometimes the messages were very old, crunchy like leaves in the fall.

Sometimes the messages were written by a quill dipped in sadness.

But most of the time they made people quite happy, for a letter can hold
the treasure of a clam-hugged pearl.

While the Uncorker of Ocean Bottles loved his job, he couldn't help
but wonder if he would ever receive a letter. Truth be told, each time
he opened a bottle, a part of him hoped to see his own name winking
from the top of the page.

But then he remembered that this was about as likely as finding a
mermaid's toenail on the beach. For he had no name. He had no
friends. He stank of seaweed and salt and fishermen's feet. No one
would ever write him a letter.

But he still would have liked it just the same.

One day, the waves tipped their white postman hats to the Uncorker and delivered a bottle with a very peculiar letter inside.

I'm not sure you will get this in time, but I am having a party.
Tomorrow, evening tide, at the seashore.
Will you please come?

"Oh dear," said the Uncorker. He had no idea who the letter was for, or where to deliver it.

But the truth was, he was very curious. He'd never been invited to a party before, and he suspected he might like to go.

First he visited the maker of cakes.

"Pardon," said the Uncorker. "But do you recognize this print?"
The cake maker studied the note.
"Don't recognize the script," he finally said. "But oh, how I love a seaside dance."

The Uncorker moved on.

He asked the candy shop owner.
He asked a woman buying chocolate-dipped treats.
He asked a young girl in a green dress.

"Sorry," each one sighed. "Though I do wish I'd received an invitation to such a party."

The Uncorker asked a seagull, a sailor, and a one-man band.
But nobody could claim the letter—nobody in the sky, or sand, or sea.

The Uncorker felt very low.
This was the first time he'd been unable to deliver a message.

As he fell asleep that night, the Uncorker decided to go to the seashore the next day. He would go, and apologize to the writer of the note.

The Uncorker of Ocean Bottles arrived early, carrying a handful of his favorite seashells. He thought it might be rude to show up uninvited and empty-handed.

The seashore was draped in seaweed and starfish. Candles floated
in clamshells. There were sand sculptures and umbrellas.

"It's you!" said the maker of cakes.
"How grand!" said the candy shop owner.
The other guests had arrived already—a woman, a girl
in a green dress, a seagull, a sailor, and a one-man band.

When the girl in green asked the Uncorker of Ocean Bottles to dance, he said,
"I'm not sure I know how, but I'd like to just the same."

As they spun across the beach, to the water's edge and back again, everyone
smiled and kept the beat.

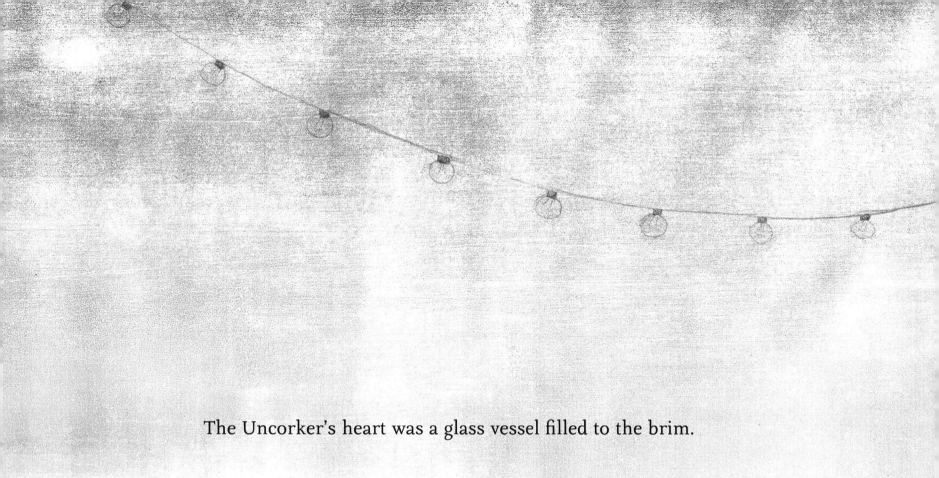

The Uncorker's heart was a glass vessel filled to the brim.

As the stars began to arrive,
and the moon as well, the Uncorker
took out the bottle he had been unable to deliver.

"Perhaps," he said, his mouth full of cake.
"Yes, perhaps I shall try to deliver this again tomorrow."